Itsy Bitsy
THE SMART SPIDER

by Charise Mericle Harper

Dial Books for Young Readers New York

THE ITSY BITSY SPIDER
WENT UP THE WATERSPOUT.

DOWN CAME THE RAIN

AND WASHED THE SPIDER OUT.

"YIKES!" SAID THE SPIDER.

"I'VE GOT TO USE MY BRAIN

AND FIGURE OUT A WAY

TO NOT GET WET AGAIN!"

SO ITSY BITSY SPIDER
CRAWLED TO THE CORNER SHOP,

SCURRIED IN THE DOOR,
THEN TO THE COUNTERTOP.

THE SPIDER ASKED THE STORE CLERK,

"MAY I SWAP THIS FLY

FOR SOME KIND OF COVER

TO KEEP ME SAFE AND DRY?"

HAPPY YAPPY STORE CLERK

JUST SHOOK HIS ITCHY HEAD.

"WELL," SAID THE SPIDER,

"HOW 'BOUT A JOB INSTEAD?"

"I CAN CATCH YOUR FLEAS AND
HELP YOU WITH THE STORE."

"FANTASTIC!" SAID THE CLERK.

"I COULDN'T ASK FOR MORE."

ITSY WENT TO WORK AND
CAUGHT ALL HAPPY'S FLEAS.

THEN SWUNG THROUGH THE STORE
SAYING "MAY I HELP YOU, PLEASE?"

SMART ITSY PUT HER STORE PAY

INSIDE A YELLOW CUP,

SAVING ALL HER MONEY

UNTIL IT WAS FILLED UP.

THEN ITSY BOUGHT HER COVER
AND SADLY SAID, "MY DEAR,

I WILL MISS YOU TRULY!"

SAD HAPPY SHED A TEAR.

HE PUT HER ON HIS HAT

AND RODE HER HOME IN STYLE,

WATCHED HER CLIMB THE SPOUT,

THEN WAITED FOR A WHILE.

ITSY SMILED AT HAPPY

AS IT BEGAN TO RAIN.

AND ITSY BITSY SPIDER...

WAS NEVER WET AGAIN!

For Ivy, who claps when I sing.
Thank you!

Published by Dial Books for Young Readers
A division of Penguin Young Readers Group
345 Hudson Street
New York, New York 10014
Copyright © 2004 by Charise Mericle Harper
Designed by Kimi Weart
Text set in James
Manufactured in China on acid-free paper

1   3   5   7   9   10   8   6   4   2

Library of Congress Cataloging-in-Publication Data
Harper, Charise Mericle.
Itsy Bitsy the smart spider / by Charise Mericle Harper.
p. cm.
Summary: The spider from the famous nursery rhyme gets a job
in order to buy a cover that will keep her dry and prevent her being
washed down the waterspout.
ISBN 0-8037-2901-4
[1. Spiders—Fiction. 2. Characters in literature—Fiction.
3. Stories in rhyme.] I. Title.
PZ8.3.H21851t 2004
[E]—dc21
2002154062

The art was created using acrylic and pencil on chipboard.